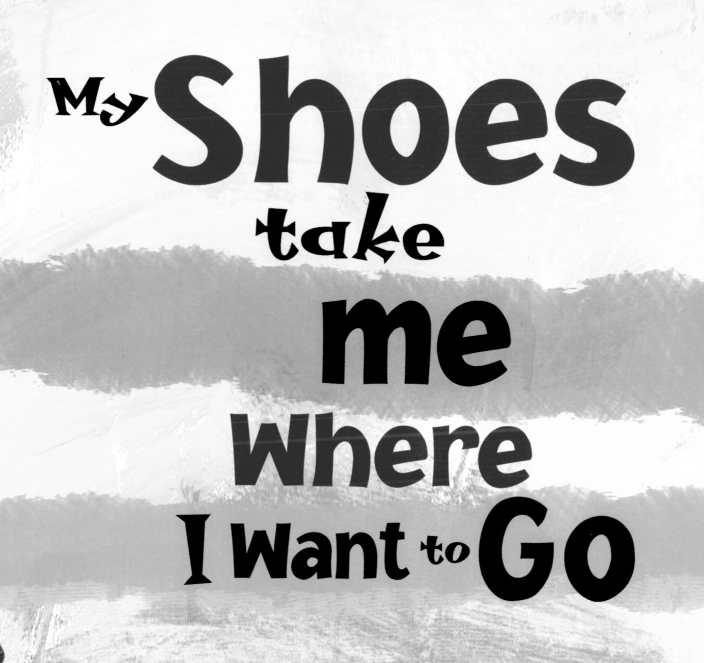

My Shoes take me Where I Want to Go

by Marianne Richmond

My Shoes take me Where I want to Go

© 2006 by Marianne Richmond Studios, Inc.

Library of Congress Control Number: 2005907882

Marianne Richmond Studios, Inc.
420 N. 5th Street, Suite 840
Minneapolis, MN 55401
www.mariannerichmond.com

ISBN 0-9753528-6-5

Illustrations by Marianne Richmond

Book design by Sara Dare Biscan

Printed in China

First Printing

My Shoes take me Where I want to Go

is dedicated to
my blue-eyed guy. — MR

When I
was born,
my mom
tells me,
I came
without
my clothes.

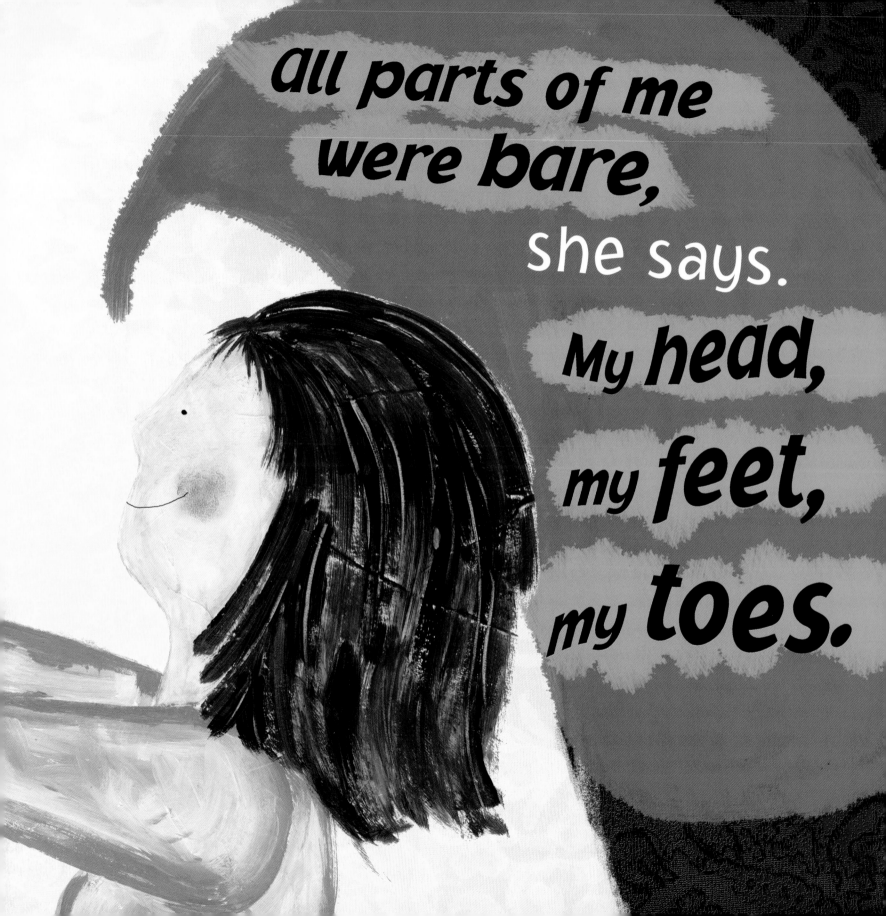

I can't imagine, I tell her,

having feet just bare,

'cause now I have all kinds of shoes

that take me everywhere!

Basketball Schedule

15

sneakers →

way to go!   yeah!!   woo-hoo!

My **sneakers** take me to the court
where I'm the **fastest pro.**

My team's behind when I **SLAM DUNK**
to cheers of

"way to go!"

My shoes that come with **bottom bumps**

3

8

make me a **soccer star.**

The tired goalie cannot rest...

↖
bottom bumps

I **score** from **near** and **far!**

My **ice skates** bring me center rink
in hockey's biggest game.

My slap shot `wins`
in overtime.

Fans **jump** and SHOUT

_**my**_ name!

On rainy days,
my red **galoshes**

take me out to sea.

I'm a **pirate**
seeking buried treasure

in lands **so far** from me.

treasure

My **sandals** take me to the beach
with waves and water grand.

With **COWBOY BOOTS** and big ol' hat,
I'm **famous** in the **WEST**

It's my **hiking boots** that lead me up **high** mountains in the air.

My **leather mocs** with fluffy fur
make me an ESKIMO.

I fish through ice for family supper
and play all day in snow!

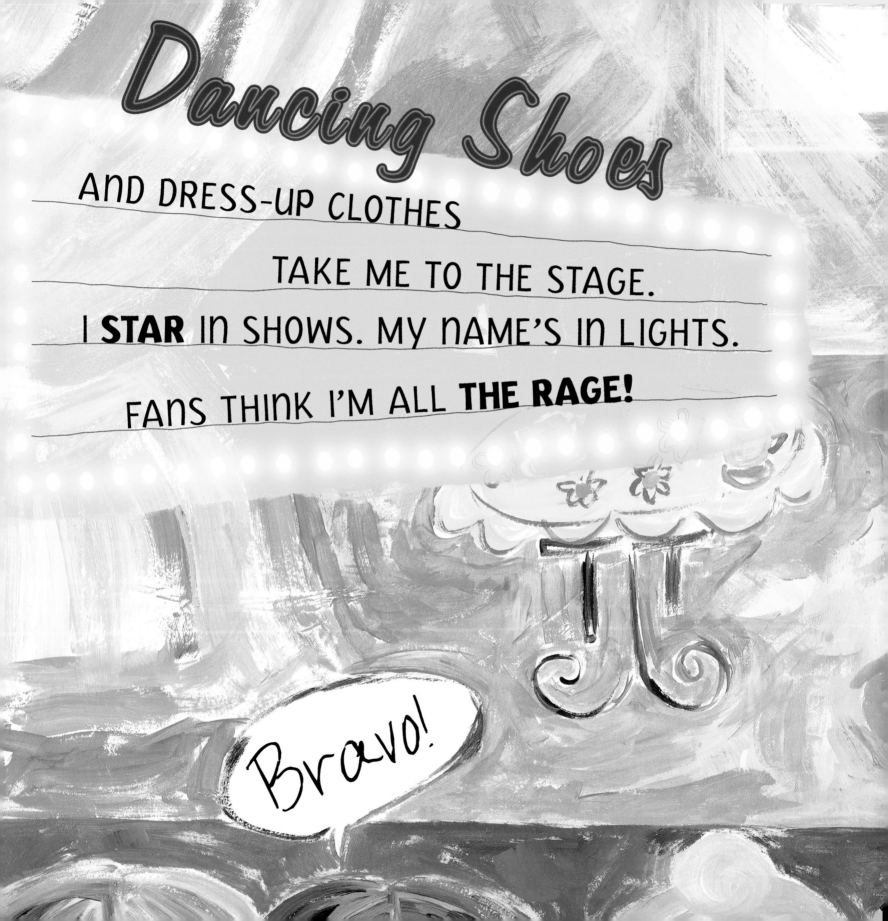

My **Sunday shoes** and cleanest pants

My Shoes take me where I want to go from where I am today.

They let me be the **different** things that I can be some day.

But when I do get tired **(yawn)** from all I do and see,

I Love You So...

my **slippers** take me to mom's lap,

where I'm *just* her *little* **me!**

slippers
quack quack

Shapes 'n
Numbers
1 2
3

The Brave Little E